This Is the Turkey

WRITTEN BY **Abby Levine**

ILLUSTRATED BY **Paige Billin-Frye**

Albert Whitman & Company

Morton Grove, Illinois

For Susannah, Sarah, and Adam. —A. L.

To Ellen and Nick. — P. B-F.

By Abby Levine and Paige Billin-Frye:

This Is the Pumpkin

Also by Abby Levine:

You Push, I Ride * What Did Mommy Do Before You?

Too Much Mush! * Ollie Knows Everything

Gretchen Groundhog, It's Your Day!

Library of Congress Cataloging-in-Publication Data

Levine, Abby.

This is the turkey / by Abby Levine; illustrated by Paige Billin-Frye.

p. cm.

Summary: Describes in humorous rhyme the activities of a young boy

and his extended family as they share a special Thanksgiving.

ISBN 0-8075-7888-6 (hardcover)

[1. Thanksgiving day—Fiction. 2. Family life—Fiction. 3. Stories in rhyme.] I. Billin-Frye, Paige, ill. II. Title.

PZ8.3.L54945 Th 2000 [E]—dc21 00-008175

The illustrations were done in watercolor, pencil, and ink.

The text typeface is Jimbo.

The design is by Scott Piehl.

This is a turkey to shout about!
And Max is the one who picked it out.

T

his is the pan where it roasts away
for the guests who are coming Thanksgiving Day.

This is the sister who kneads the bread
as Dad stirs the cranberries, ruby-red,
while the turkey is roasting away
for the guests who are coming Thanksgiving Day.

This is the uncle with salad greens;
this is the aunt with her famous beans
who kisses the sister, admires the bread,
and praises the cranberries, ruby-red,
while sniffing the turkey that's roasting away
for the guests who are coming Thanksgiving Day.

T

hese are the cousins who come to play
with Max and his sister Thanksgiving Day.

These are the neighbors, their arms piled high
with cookies and brownies and pumpkin pie.

This is a turkey to shout about!
And soon Max's mother will take it out!

This is the broccoli (quite a lot!),
this is the stuffing, piping hot.
These are the cranberries, ruby-red,
the yams, the gravy, the homemade bread.
This is the table, beautifully spread!

This is a turkey to shout about!
Crispy and golden and—

YIKES!—

WATCH

This is the grandma who says, "Max, dear, we have all we need because everyone's here."

This is the grandpa who takes his seat.
"No turkey? No problem! I'm hungry—

Let's eat!"

T

his is the thanks for all that's good:
home and family and friends and food.

This is the time to pass salad greens,
a heaping bowlful of famous beans,
bunches of broccoli in a pot,
savory stuffing, piping hot,
oceans of cranberries, ruby-red,
yams and gravy and homemade bread,
and—after a little time's gone by—
cookies and brownies and pumpkin pie!

These are the games and this is the fun,
after Thanksgiving dinner is done.

These are the guests as they go away;

this is the end of a happy day.

This is Max, who says, "I bet we had the best Thanksgiving yet!"